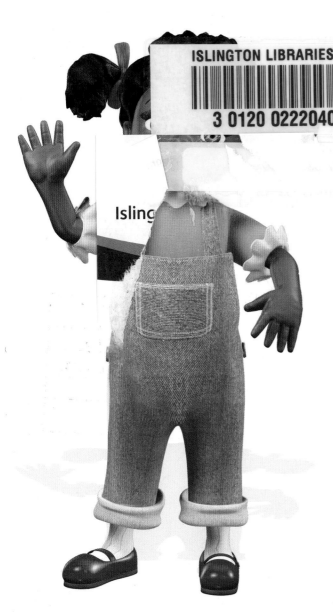

D__ah Doll

HarperCollins *Children's Books*

Dinah Doll was very happy.
She had spent a few days in the
countryside, and was feeling rested.
Arriving back at Toy Town station,
she gave a little skip and thought
how much she was looking forward
to returning to her stall and seeing
all of her friends again.

However, while Dinah Doll
had been away, the Goblins
had been using her stall
to get up to bad tricks.

The Goblins had pretended to everyone
in Toy Town that Dinah had left them
in charge of the stall! Everyone had
believed the Goblins and bought
all sorts of things from them.

The two naughty Goblins had just sold Clockwork Clown a bouncing ball that had lost its bounce, when Dinah Doll appeared, whistling a happy tune.

"Quick, Sly! Scarper!" hissed Gobbo as he heard Dinah whistling.

Quick as a flash, the Goblins ran off before Dinah saw them. Not knowing anything had been amiss while she was away, Dinah Doll set up her stall so it was tidy and ready for customers.

Before long, her first customer appeared.

"Hello, Mr Sparks!" greeted
Dinah Doll with a smile.

"Hello, Dinah," he replied, unhappily.
"I have come to complain about the nuts
and bolts I bought from you. They have
all broken already! I expect you to only
sell good quality nuts and bolts."

Poor Dinah. She did only sell good quality
nuts and bolts. Something must be wrong.

Before Dinah Doll could answer Mr Sparks,
Noddy came running up to the stall.

"Dinah, I was just about to make some
googleberry muffins for Skippy Skittle's
birthday when I found that the eggs I bought
from you were bad! Now I won't be able
to make the muffins in time!" gasped Noddy,
who was out of breath from all that running.

Dinah scratched her head. She only
ever sold the freshest eggs available.
Why were Noddy's eggs bad?

Dinah Doll didn't have a moment
to wonder what had been going
on before Miss Pink Cat came up.
She was not looking very happy, either.

"Dinah Doll!" cried Miss Pink Cat. "When I buy
my milk from you, I expect it to be fresh!
I cannot make ice cream with milk that has got
lumpy bits in it! So I cannot make ice cream
today! What are you going to do about it?"

Dinah Doll frowned. She certainly
never sells milk that has turned sour!

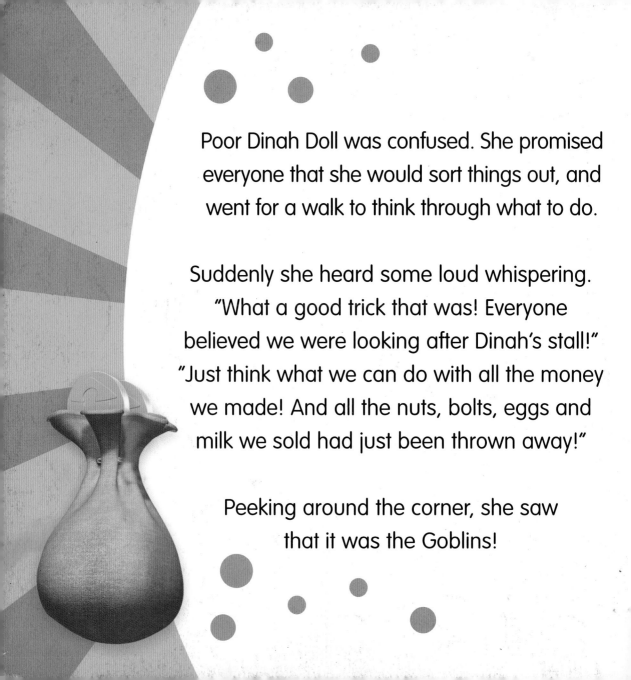

Poor Dinah Doll was confused. She promised everyone that she would sort things out, and went for a walk to think through what to do.

Suddenly she heard some loud whispering. "What a good trick that was! Everyone believed we were looking after Dinah's stall!" "Just think what we can do with all the money we made! And all the nuts, bolts, eggs and milk we sold had just been thrown away!"

Peeking around the corner, she saw that it was the Goblins!

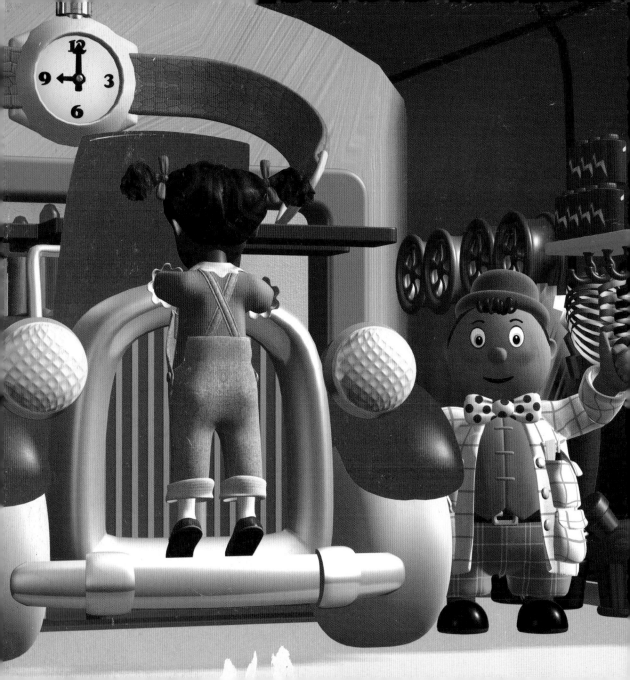

Dinah Doll knew she had
to put everything right.

First, she brought brand new
nuts and bolts to Mr Sparks' garage.

"I'm so sorry, Mr Sparks," she apologised.
"Let me make it up to you by fitting these
brand new nuts and bolts for you," Dinah
offered. "I know a thing or two about cars…"

"Thank you," replied Mr Sparks.

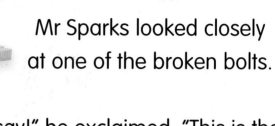

Mr Sparks looked closely
at one of the broken bolts.

"I say!" he exclaimed. "This is the very
same bolt I threw out last week
because it had broken!"

"So the Goblins took nuts and bolts you
had already thrown away, and sold them
back to you!" Dinah realised.

Dinah had put things right with Mr Sparks,
but had more customers to see.

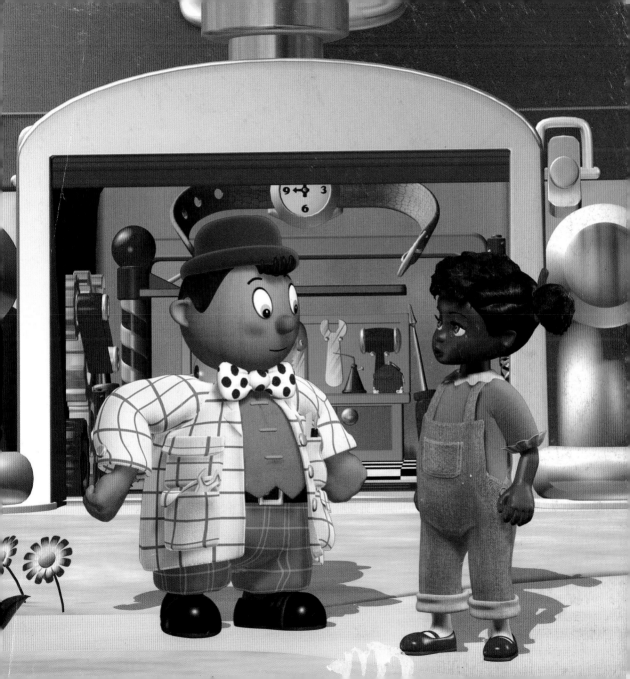

Next, Dinah took a basket
of fresh eggs to Noddy.

"Noddy, I am so sorry that the Goblins
sold you bad eggs," said Dinah Doll.
"Please accept this basket of fresh eggs
as an apology. Look! They are still
warm from the hens!"

"Oh, thank you, Dinah. That is very kind.
I will bring you a googleberry muffin as soon
as they are out of the oven!" promised
Noddy, who was now happy again.

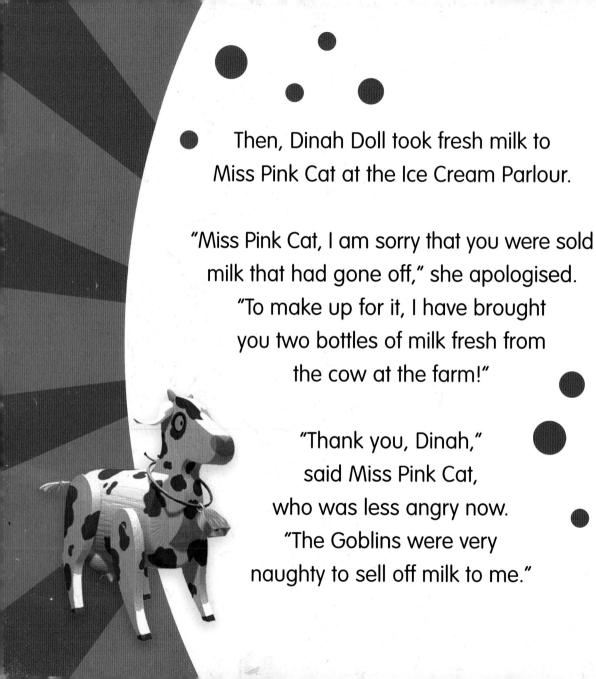

Then, Dinah Doll took fresh milk to
Miss Pink Cat at the Ice Cream Parlour.

"Miss Pink Cat, I am sorry that you were sold
milk that had gone off," she apologised.
"To make up for it, I have brought
you two bottles of milk fresh from
the cow at the farm!"

"Thank you, Dinah,"
said Miss Pink Cat,
who was less angry now.
"The Goblins were very
naughty to sell off milk to me."

Dinah had put things right with Mr Sparks, Noddy and Miss Pink Cat. But she was still worried that the Goblins had upset all of her customers.

The last thing Dinah Doll wanted was upset customers!

There was one last thing for Dinah Doll to put right. The Goblins had to learn a lesson, and return the money to Dinah. And so Dinah Doll went to make a plan with Mr Plod. Mr Plod hid behind her stall and waited…

Before long, the Goblins came up to
the stall. "Hello, Dinah," sneered Gobbo.
"Did you have a good holiday?"

"Yes, thank you," she replied.
"But my customers were not
at all happy with the bad
things that you sold them!"

"I don't know what
you are talking about!"
replied Sly, trying
to sound innocent.

Suddenly, Mr Plod sprang
out from behind the stall.

"Halt in the name of Plod!
I arrest you two Goblins for
the unlawful sale of broken
nuts and bolts and bad
eggs and milk!"

And with that, Mr Plod took
the two grumbling Goblins to jail.

Dinah Doll was delighted to
have her stall back to normal.
Just one thing was still not right…

Mr Plod ran up to her.
"Your missing money, Dinah!"
he said, as he gave her
a bag full of golden coins.

"Everything is put right now,
Mr Plod! Thank you!"
she smiled.

First published in the UK by HarperCollins Children's Books in 2008

1 3 5 7 9 10 8 6 4 2

ISBN-13: 978-0-00-727814-5

ISBN-10: 0-00-727814-4

Printed and bound in China

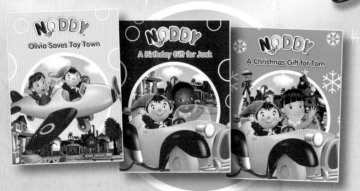